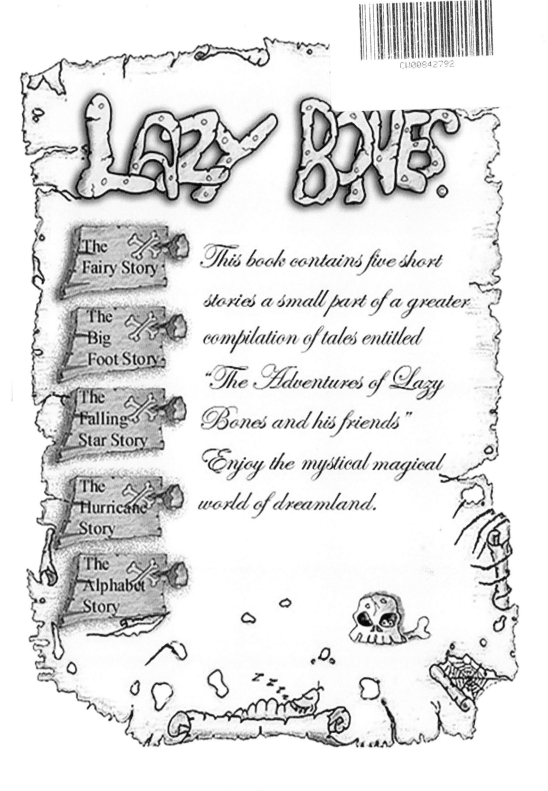

LAZY BONES

The Fairy Story

The Big Foot Story

The Falling Star Story

The Hurricane Story

The Alphabet Story

This book contains five short stories a small part of a greater compilation of tales entitled "The Adventures of Lazy Bones and his friends" Enjoy the mystical magical world of dreamland.

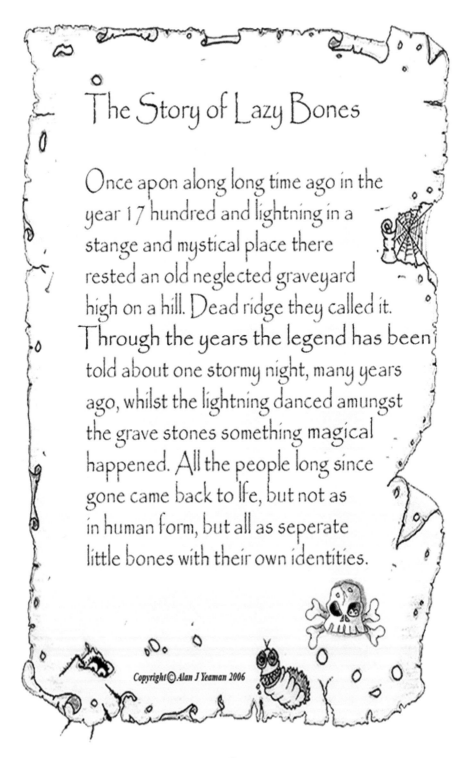

The Story of Lazy Bones

Once apon along long time ago in the year 17 hundred and lightning in a stange and mystical place there rested an old neglected graveyard high on a hill. Dead ridge they called it. Through the years the legend has been told about one stormy night, many years ago, whilst the lightning danced amungst the grave stones something magical happened. All the people long since gone came back to lfe, but not as in human form, but all as seperate little bones with their own identities.

Thus was born Lazy Bones and his companions, Skull, Hippy, Spiney, and Spare Ribs. They all danced with their new found friends, Handy, Footsie and Funny Bones laughed till the tear rolled down his face.

It was a truly magical happening. Worlds apart from the human race and still to this very day you can go to the cemetery high on the hill in the middle of the night and if you are very quiet you will see Lazy Bones and his friends playing amongst the old tombstones.

The Magical Happening

The Fairy Story...
One still and silent night Citizen Lazy Bones was taking a stroll
through the graveyard. He was dressed up like a king. With crown,
bright jewels and all the other royal regalia.

Lurking in the shadows of the old gravestones stooped Wicked
Witch Skull and her companions Convict skull and Mummy Skull
near by.

Without warning Wicked Witch Skull and her two cronies Mummy Skull and Convict Skull attacked Citizen Lazy Bones. They tied Lazy Bones up against a grave stone with length of old rope.

Just as the three baddies are mocking helpless Lazy Bones a good fairy appears from nowere. The good fairy zaps the evil threesome with her magic wand. But before Lazy Bones could thank the good Fairy...

The scary hairy spider drops on to *Lazy Bones* bed
and awakens him, just to find he was only dreaming.

Big FOOT Story...
*Citizen Spare Ribs has discovered very large foot prints in the ground
and runs to tell the others. Citizen Skull decides to bring in Inspector
Skull to investigate.*

The trail of the enormous foot prints leads them to the old church.
"It must be a giant" said Inspector Skull. "We had better call in
Colonel Skull for back up".

They all surrounded the old church in a bid to force the monster out. Suddenly the old church door creeked open to reveal a harmless little green Martian with enormous feet. They all fell about laughing.

The little green Martian tells his story about his broken down flying saucer. Professor Skull and the Lab Bones go to work on repairing the flying machine.

...and the happy little green martian continued on his journey into the night sky.

The falling star story...
One clear still night as Professor Skull is observing the night sky
with his telescope. He sees a falling star heading straight for the
graveyard. He immediately tells the others.

They all gather round looking in amazment as the little Star lit up their faces. Then it began to fade, it was dying. They tried to think of a way...

to save it. "I know who can save the Star" said Miner Skull. Then he promptly disappeared down one of his many tunnels.

...and returned with Captain Skull and the Pirate Bones pulling a large cannon. "Where do you want it me hearties?" asked Captain Skull waving his cutlass in the air.

The Professor pointed to the empty space in the sky. "Up there" He said aloud. The Pirates aimed the huge cannon in that direction and with a mighty bang the little star was back up in the night sky once more and twice as bright

Wicked Witch Skull is making up another magic spell. She's brewing up a hurricane which she stuffs into a velvet bag tied with a golden cord and...

18

...sent Convict Skull down to the graveyard, with instructions to leave the bag in an open space so the little bones would pick it up and investigate the contents.

Citizen Hippie finds the bag and hurries back to the others with his booty. "Look what I found everybody it must be treasure!!" he said with excitement.

The little bones enthusiastically opened the bag
releasing the hurricane!!!.

Copyright © Alan J Yeaman 2006

Wizard Funny Bones runs to tell Wizard Skull about all the commotion in the graveyard.

Wizard Skull reverses the spell and puts the hurricane back in the bag, then...

...He connects it to a drain pipe on the Witches castle and sends the hurricane back to the Wicked Witch. All the little bones fell about laughing.

The Alphabet Story...
Wicked Witch Skull is up to her tricks once more. She is
making a magic brew which brings all the letters of the ...

Alphabet to life!!!

The bad Witch Skull sent all the wicked words down to the graveyard causing chaos and sending all the little bones...

running for their lives.

As the Witches spell faded away and the graveyard returned to its normal tranquility. Professor Skull asked some of the...

little bones to gather up all the words scattered around the graveyard.

They put all the words into a large pot and made them into Alphabet soup.
All the little bones sat round the table chatting and laughing into the night.

THE END

LAZY BONES

"Please take notice that the enclosed material in this book consisting of 28 pages of drawings and associated text entitled *Lazy Bones*, is the copyright of Alan J. Yeaman and all rights are reserved"

contact ajyeaman@outlook.com

Printed in Great Britain
by Amazon

26007748R00018